WALT DISNEY PRODUCTIONS

presents

A Scare for Mr. Toad

Book Club Edition

Random House 🏠 **New York**

Copyright © 1985 by Walt Disney Productions. All rights reserved under International and Pan-American Copyright Conventions. Published in the United States by Random House, Inc., New York, and simultaneously in Canada by Random House of Canada Limited, Toronto. ISBN: 0-394-87586-9 Manufactured in the United States of America
567890 ABCDEFGHIJK

Mr. Toad of Toad Hall was bored.

He had nowhere to go and nothing to do.

He had crashed all his cars.

He had smashed all his bicycles.

And he hadn't even paid for them yet!

"I wish I had some visitors," said Toad.

"I know!" said Toad. "I'll invite Rat
and Mole to tea tomorrow."

He went inside to his study to write
to his friends.

Dear Rat and Mole,
Please come to tea tomorrow.
We will have wonderful treats.
Toad

"I will mail the invitation myself,"
Toad said.

"I'm going to the post office," Toad called upstairs.

MacBadger, Toad's old friend and business manager, was working up there.

"Umpf," said MacBadger.

He was very busy paying Toad's bills.

Toad had many, many bills!

On the way out, Toad passed
MacBadger's bike.

"Hmm," said Toad. "It's a long way
to the post office. I think I'll ride."

"MacBadger, I need your bike!" called Toad.

"No, Toad! There's something the matter with the brakes. Just leave the bike alone," said MacBadger.

But Toad
loved wheels.

"Who needs brakes?" he thought.
"Not a terrific rider like me!"
When MacBadger's
back was turned,
Toad hopped
on the bike.

MacBadger was right.
There WAS something the matter
with the brakes.
They didn't work at all.
But Toad did not care.

He loved a fast ride.
Everything went fine
until . . .

...Toad crossed
a bridge and...

ran into a flock of sheep just where
Mole and Rat were fishing.

CRUNCH! CRASH! went the bike.

"Yikes!" said Toad, Mole, and Rat.

No one was hurt.

But the bike was ruined.

"Hello, chaps!" said Toad. "I was coming to invite you to tea tomorrow."

"Toad, wasn't that MacBadger's bike?" asked Rat.

"It was," said Toad. "But it wasn't any good. I'll get him a new one."

And he walked away with the ruined bike.

"Toad is being very careless," said Rat. "MacBadger will be angry when he sees the bike."

MacBadger was waiting
when Toad got home.
And MacBadger was angry.

"I told you not to take my bike!"
cried MacBadger. "You took it anyway.
And you ruined it! How could you!"

"So sorry, old chap, but don't worry,"
said Toad. "I'll buy you a new bike.
You know I'm good for the money."

"Money!" said MacBadger. "You think
that money takes care of everything!
It is time you learned better."
And he stomped off to his office.

MacBadger tried to go
back to work.
But he was too angry.

"So Toad thinks he can just help
himself to my things and then pay
me off!" fumed MacBadger. "Why,
the nerve of him! I've had it!"

MacBadger packed up and left Toad Hall.
"You are no friend of mine, Toad,"
said MacBadger. "You are rude and selfish.
Get yourself another business manager.
I quit."

Toad watched MacBadger
trudge down the road.
"What a sourpuss he is,"
said Toad. "He'll be back
as soon as he cools off."

But MacBadger did not come back.
"Oh, who needs him!" said Toad.
"I'll be my own business manager."
And he went upstairs to the office.

Toad began to go through his bills.
He could not make sense out of them.

Then the phone
started ringing.
"You'll get your
money!" Toad told
the callers. "Just
give me time!"

Soon Toad was
all worn out.
And he still
had not paid
one bill.

"Oh, I'm so confused," said Toad.
He threw the bills in the air and
walked out of the office.

Days passed.
But MacBadger
did not return.
And the bills
were still unpaid.

Toad began to feel sorry for himself.
"MacBadger is being mean to me," he said.

"It isn't fair," said Toad.
"MacBadger knows how much I need him.
I am really cross with him.
I'm going to tell Rat and Mole."
Toad grabbed his hat and marched out.

First Toad walked down to Mole's house.

He knocked at the door.
But no one answered.

Then Toad went over to Rat's house on the river.

But no one was home there, either.

"I wonder if Rat and Mole went to visit MacBadger," said Toad.

So Toad set off for MacBadger's place in the Wild Wood.

Toad walked and walked.
It was a long way to the Wild Wood.

Finally Toad reached it.
By then, the sun was setting.

The woods were dark and scary.
They were full of wild noises and
bright eyes.

Strange things swooped through the air.

Soon Toad was terrified.
"Oh, I hope I can find MacBadger,"
he moaned. "Then I'll be nice to him
forever!"

Deep in the woods, Mole and Rat were with MacBadger in his cozy home.

They were drinking tea and talking about selfish Mr. Toad.

Suddenly there was a knock at the door.

A faint voice
called, "Help! Help!
Let me in!"
"Someone is in
trouble out there,"
said Mole. "I'll
see who it is."
And he went
to open the door.

There was
Toad!

"Oh, Moley!" cried Toad. "I've had
such a scare!"
"Hello, Toad. I'm glad to see you,"
said Mole. "So you have finally come
to apologize to MacBadger."

"Apologize?" said Toad.

Toad had not thought about apologizing.
But he knew that was exactly what
he had to do.

"Here is Toad to see you, MacBadger,"
said Mole.

MacBadger eyed Toad.
What was the rascal up to now?
"Oh, MacBadger, my dear old friend,"
began Toad. "Can you ever forgive me?"

"I am so very sorry I took your bike,"
Toad went on. "It was very wrong of me.
I don't know what came over me.
I have no excuse. I behaved very badly.
I am the lowest of toads."

"Please come back to Toad Hall,
MacBadger. I need you!" said Toad.

"Humph!" said MacBadger.
But he was glad to hear Toad's apology.

Toad kept begging MacBadger to come back.
"I will think about it," said MacBadger.
Then Ratty rowed Toad home on the river.

"I expect MacBadger will come back,"
said Ratty. "He was getting bored at home.
But you will really have to behave better,
Toad."

"Oh, I will," said Toad.
"I've learned my lesson.
I promise."

The next day
MacBadger went
to Toad Hall.

Toad had a brand-new bike for him.
"I broke your bike and you MUST
let me replace it," said Toad.

MacBadger only grunted,
but he looked pleased.

He went up to the office . . .

. . . and was soon
hard at work
on the bills.

Toad watched him happily.
"Anything I can do to help?"
asked Toad after a while.
"Why, yes. You can take these
paid bills to the post office,"
said MacBadger.
"Gladly," said Toad.

On the way out, Toad passed
MacBadger's new bike.

"It would be so much faster
to ride," thought Toad.

He looked up at the office.

MacBadger was looking down
at Toad.

"Better not!" thought Toad.

Toad set off down the drive.

"Maybe I'll ride the bike tomorrow," Toad said to himself. "After all, I paid for it! MacBadger shouldn't mind."

Oh, Mr. Toad!